U0022533

For Obi

Speedy the Greedy Turtle

貪吃的烏龜小快

Jill McDougall 著

王祖民 繪

三民

Speedy the turtle lived in a glass *tank by the window.
He was a very greedy turtle. He liked to eat *peas.
He liked to eat corn. He liked to eat *snails and *worms.

*為生字，請參照生字表

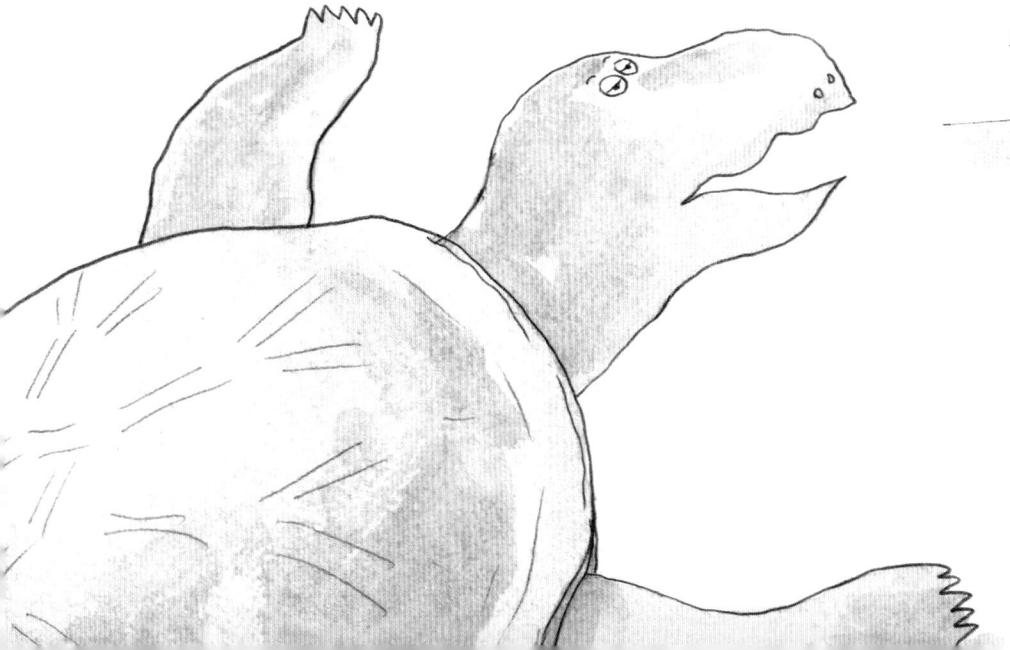

And he liked

to eat them all at the same time.

"Speedy looks very fat," said Julie one day.

"Yes, he does," said Dad.

"We must take him to the *vet."

Dad carried Speedy's
glass tank all the way down the
street to the vet. Mom and Julie came too.

"Mmm," said the vet. "This turtle is getting too much food. There will be no more *treats for Speedy."

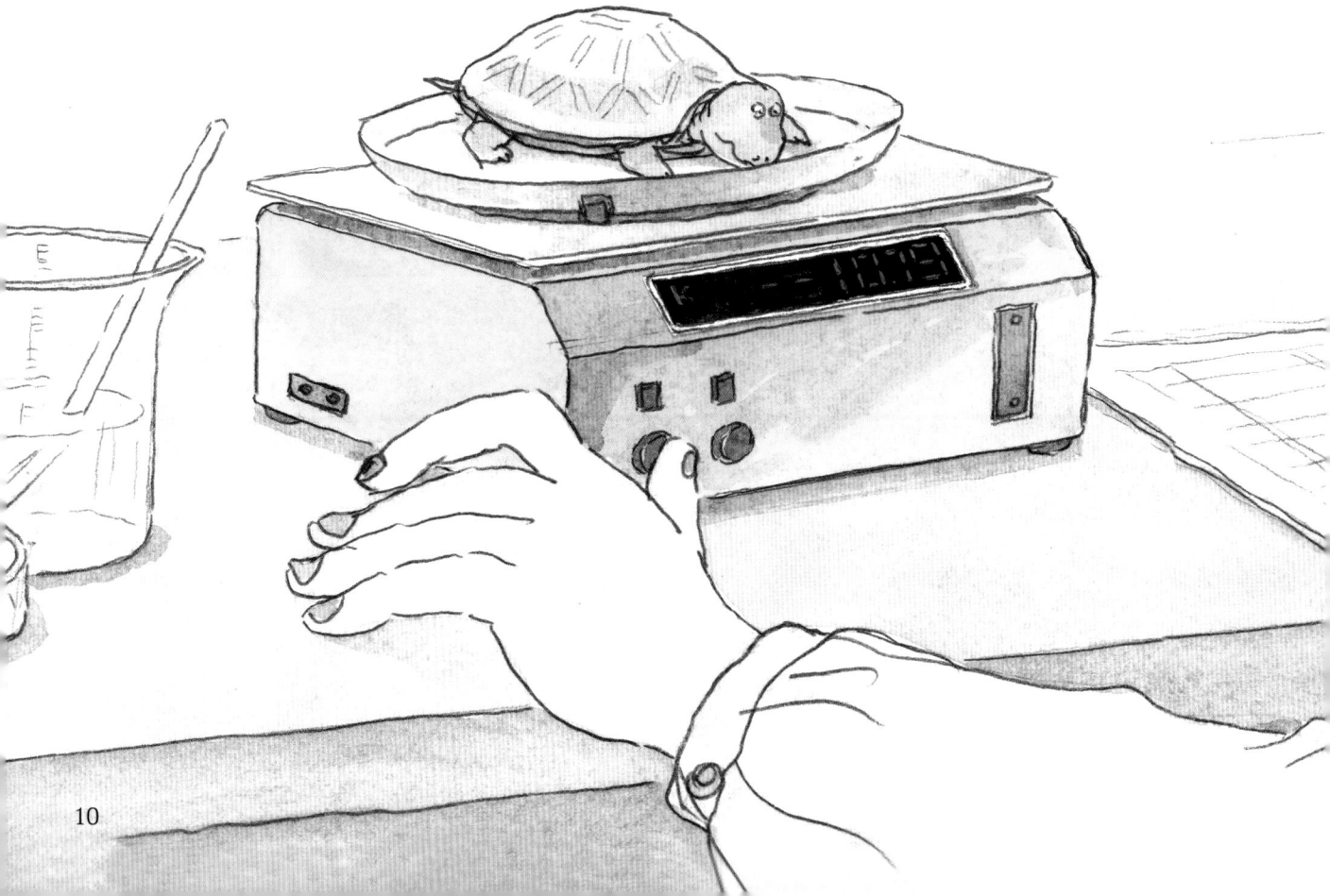

"Fine," said Julie. "No more treats for Speedy."

"Okay," said Mom.

"No more treats for Speedy."

"That's right," said Dad.

"No more treats for Speedy."

That night, Julie gave Speedy two small snails for dinner. "That's all," said Julie. "You are getting much too fat."

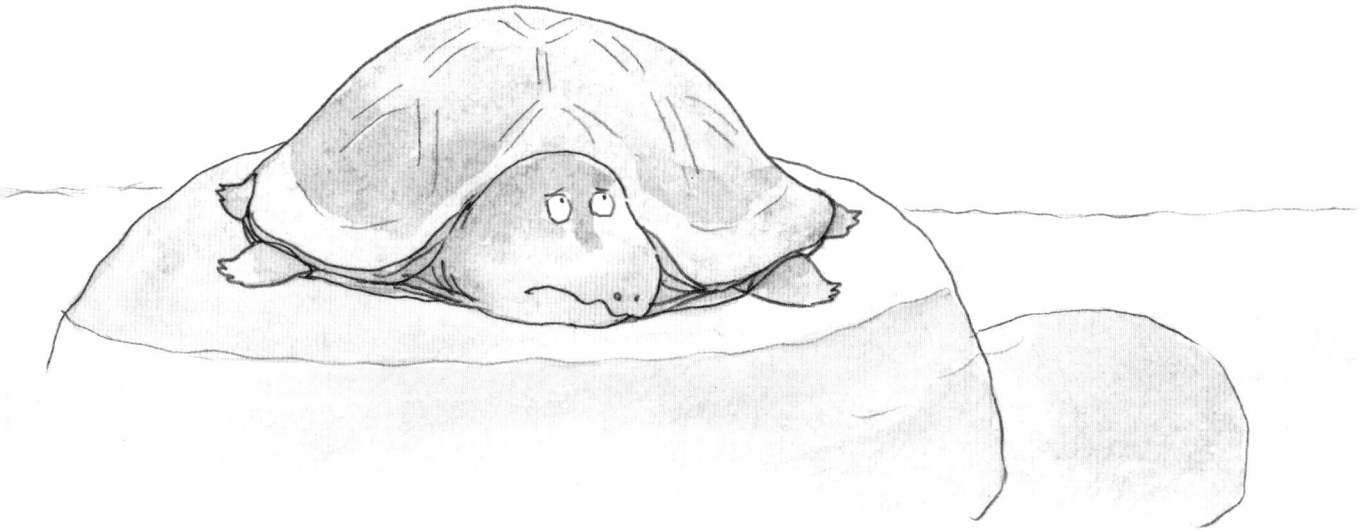

Speedy looked back at Julie with his little brown eyes. He *seemed very sad.

Later on, Dad *crept over to Speedy's glass home.

"Poor Speedy," said Dad. "Are you hungry?"

He gave Speedy a worm.

"One little worm won't matter," said Dad.

Speedy looked back at Dad with his little brown eyes.

He *still seemed very sad.

Later still, Mom crept in to see Speedy.

"Poor Speedy," said Mom. "You look very hungry."

She gave Speedy some peas.

"A few little peas won't matter," said Mom.

Speedy looked back at Mom with his little brown eyes. He still seemed very sad.

When Mom and Dad were in bed, Julie crept in to see Speedy.

"Poor Speedy," said Julie. "Are you very hungry?"

She gave Speedy some corn. "One little bit of corn won't matter," said Julie.

Speedy looked back at Julie with his little brown eyes. He still seemed very sad.

A few days later, Mom and Dad and Julie came to look at Speedy. He was sitting on a rock and he looked very very fat.

"Oh dear," said Julie. "Speedy is fatter than ever."

She put Speedy on her hand and turned him over.
"Look at that fat *belly," said Julie. "No more treats for Speedy."

"Okay," said Mom. "No more treats for Speedy."

"That's right," said Dad. "No more treats for Speedy."

Julie put Speedy back in his glass case.

"Poor Speedy," said Dad.

"Poor Speedy," said Julie.

“Poor Speedy,” said Mom.

Speedy looked back at them with his little brown eyes. He seemed to be *smiling.

生字表

greedy [`gridɪ] adj. 貪吃的

p.3

tank [tæŋk] n. (用來盛裝液體的) 箱，槽

pea [pi] n. 豌豆

snail [snel] n. 蝸牛

worm [wɝm] n. (無足的) 蟲

p.7

vet [vɛt] n. 獸醫

p.10

treat [trit] n. 原指請客、款待，這裡引申為烏龜小快喜歡吃的東西

p.15

seem [sim] v. 似乎，看起來好像

p.16

creep [krip] v. 躡手躡腳的走，悄悄靠近

still [stɪl] adv. 仍然，還是

p.24

belly [`bɛlɪ] n. 腹部，肚子

p.28

smile [smaɪl] v. 微笑

adj.= 形容詞， adv.= 副詞， n.= 名詞， v.= 動詞

故事中譯

p.3

烏龜小快住在窗戶旁的玻璃箱裡。他是一隻非常貪吃的烏龜。他喜歡吃豌豆；他喜歡吃玉米；他喜歡吃蝸牛和小蟲。

p.4-5

而且，他喜歡同時把它們一起吃掉。

p.6

有一天，茱莉說：「小快看起來好肥喔！」

p.7

爸爸說：「沒錯，他的確是很肥。我們得帶他去看獸醫才行。」

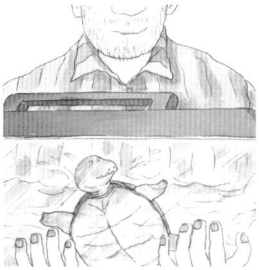

p.9

爸爸帶著小快的玻璃箱，一路走到街道的另一頭去找獸醫。媽媽和茱莉也跟著去了。

p.10

獸醫說：「嗯，這隻烏龜吃太多食物了，不能再亂餵小快吃東西了。」

p.12-13

茱莉說：「好。以後不會再亂餵小快吃東西了。」

媽媽說：「是的！不會再亂餵小快吃東西了。」

爸爸說：「沒錯！不會再亂餵小快吃東西了。」

p.14

那天晚上，茱莉給小快兩隻小蝸牛當晚餐。她說：「晚餐就只有這樣。你實在變得太肥了。」

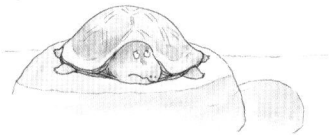

p.15

小快回過頭用他那小小的棕色眼睛看著茱莉，看起來很傷心的樣子。

p.16

過了一會兒，爸爸悄悄的走到小快的玻璃箱旁。他說：「可憐的小快。你餓了嗎？」他給了小快一條蟲吃，然後說：「只是一條小蟲，應該沒關係的。」小快回過頭用他小小的棕色眼睛看著爸爸，看起來還是很傷心的樣子。

p.19

又過了一會兒，媽媽悄悄的來看小快。她說：「可憐的小快。你看起來很餓。」她給了小快一些豌豆吃，然後說：「只是幾顆小小的豌豆，應該沒關係的。」

小快回過頭用他那小小的棕色眼睛看著媽媽，仍舊是一副很傷心的樣子。

p.20

媽媽和爸爸上床睡覺後，茱莉悄悄的來看小快。茱莉說：「可憐的小快。你是不是很餓呢？」她給了小快一些玉米吃，然後說：「只是一點點玉米，應該沒關係的。」

小快回過頭用他那小小的棕色眼睛看著茱莉，還是一副很傷心的樣子。

p.22

幾天之後，媽媽、爸爸和茱莉一起來看小快。小快正坐在一塊石頭上，他看起來很肥很肥。

茱莉說：「喔！天啊！小快比以前更肥了。」

p.24

她把小快放在手上，然後把他翻過來。茱莉說：「看看他的肥肚子，以後真的不要再亂餵小快吃東西了。」

媽媽說：「是的！真的不要再亂餵小快吃東西了。」

爸爸說：「沒錯！真的不要再亂餵小快吃東西了。」

p.26-27

茱莉把小快放回他的玻璃箱裡。

爸爸說：「可憐的小快。」

茱莉說：「可憐的小快。」

媽媽說：「可憐的小快。」

p.28

小快回過頭用他那小小的棕色眼睛看著他們，他好像正在微笑呢。

句型練習解答

(2) Jeff likes to eat apples.
Mon likes to eat potatoes.
I don't like to eat carrots.
She doesn't like to eat fish.
Tina likes to eat cake.
Children like to eat ice cream.
Kelly likes to eat sandwiches.
He doesn't like to eat tomatoes.

句型練習

Someone Likes to Eat....

在「貪吃的烏龜小快快」故事中，有很多關於"Speedy likes to eat...."（小快喜歡吃……）的用法，現在我們就一起來練習"Someone likes to eat...."（某人喜歡吃……）的句型吧！

① 請跟著 CD 的 Track 4，唸出下面這些「食物」的英文單字：

apples

fish

cake

sandwiches

tomatoes

carrots

potatoes

ice cream

② 請仔細聽 CD 的 Track 5，利用左頁的單字提示完成以下的句子：

Speedy likes to eat peas.

Speedy likes to eat corn.

Speedy likes to eat snails.

Speedy likes to eat worms.

Jeff likes to eat _____.

Mom likes to eat _____.

I don't like to eat _____.

She doesn't like to eat _____.

Tina likes to eat _____.

Children like to eat _____.

Kelly likes to eat _____.

He doesn't like to eat _____.

認識烏龜

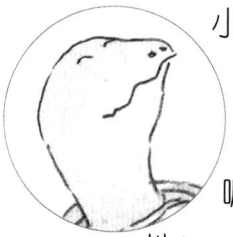

小朋友，你知道嗎？故事中的烏龜小快是屬於爬蟲類呢！牠是一隻紅耳龜，又稱赤耳龜或巴西龜，不過，牠可不是從巴西來的喔！牠的故鄉在美國東南部及墨西哥等地。紅耳龜是半水棲性的動物，因為有著超強的適應力和討喜可愛的外型，通常被當作寵物飼養。現在就讓我們來看看，紅耳龜的外型有哪些獨特的地方吧！

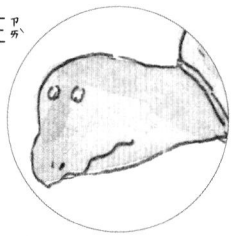

「紅耳龜」，顧名思義，就是牠們在兩側眼睛後面，各有一條亮麗又搶眼的紅色耳斑（有些看起來是橘色的），這是牠們最明顯的特徵。此外，紅耳龜沒有牙齒，不過牠們的嘴巴很硬，上顎的邊緣非常銳利，可以用來咬斷植物；而在吃肉的時候，牠們會用前腳將食物踩住，把肉撕開來吃。

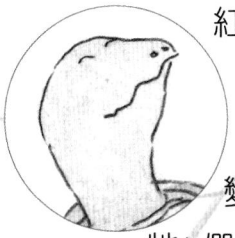

紅耳龜小時候的殼是翠綠色，上面還有漂亮的黃綠花紋，乍看之下很像西瓜皮呢！但隨著年齡增長，殼的顏色會漸漸變得黯淡，成為較深的橄欖綠。如果你把牠們翻過來觀察，會發現牠們的肚皮是黃色的喔！

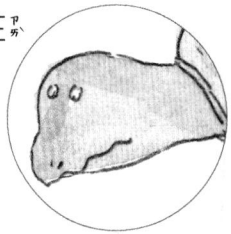

紅耳龜的腳掌間有蹼，讓牠們方便在水裡游泳。在牠們長到約十公分大小的時候，你會發現雄龜的前腳爪會比雌龜的前腳爪細長，而且雄龜的尾巴會比較長，尾巴根部也會比較粗一點。

紅耳龜是雜食性動物，幾乎什麼都吃，所以最大可以長到二十到三十公分。牠們喜歡吃小魚、甲殼類及軟體動物，也愛吃植物和果實。其實，年幼的紅耳龜偏肉食性，年紀越大，牠們就越喜歡多吃些植物類的食物，這也難怪故事中的小快會長得這麼「健康壯碩」了！

寫書的人

Jill McDougall is an Australian children's writer whose first book, "Anna the Goanna," was a Children's Book Council Notable Book. Jill has written and published over eighty titles for children including short stories, picture books and novels. Jill enjoys yoga, cooking and walking her two dogs along the beach.

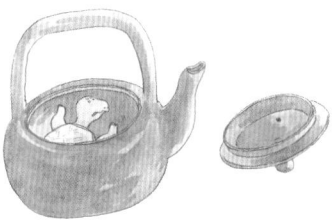

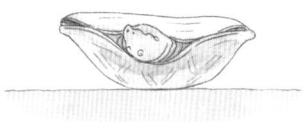

畫畫的人

王祖民，江蘇蘇州市人。現任江蘇少年兒童出版社美術編輯副編審，從事兒童讀物插圖創作工作，作品曾多次在國際國內獲獎。作品《虎丘山》曾獲聯合國科教文野間兒童讀物插圖獎。

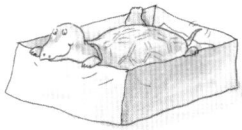

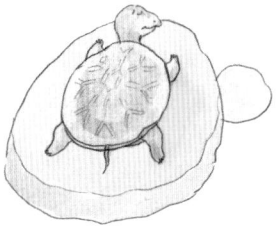

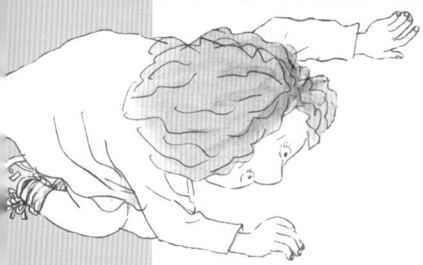

小烏龜大麻煩系列
Turtle Trouble Series

Jill McDougall　著／王祖民　繪

附中英雙語朗讀CD／適合具基礎英文閱讀能力者(國小4-6年級)閱讀

① 貪吃的烏龜小快 **(Speedy the Greedy Turtle)**
② 小快的比賽 **(Speedy's Race)**
③ 小快上學去 **(Speedy Goes to School)**
④ 電視明星小快 **(Speedy the TV Star)**
⑤ 怎麼啦，小快？ **(What's Wrong, Speedy?)**
⑥ 小快在哪裡？ **(Where Is Speedy?)**

烏龜小快是小女孩茱莉養的寵物，他既懶散又貪吃，還因此鬧出不少笑話，讓茱莉一家人的生活充滿歡笑跟驚奇！想知道烏龜小快發生了什麼事嗎？快看《小烏龜大麻煩系列》故事，保證讓你笑聲不斷喔！

活潑可愛的插畫
還有突破傳統的編排方式
視覺效果令人耳目一新

幽默的文字，簡單的句型，
不會造成閱讀負擔

故事中譯保持英文原味，又可當成完整的中文故事閱讀

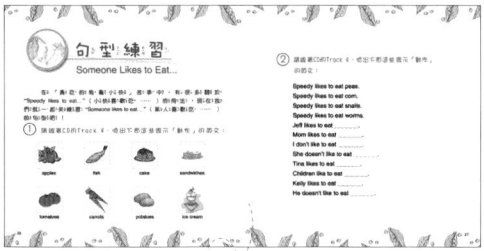

書後附英文句型練習，加強讀者應用句型能力，幫助讀者融會貫通

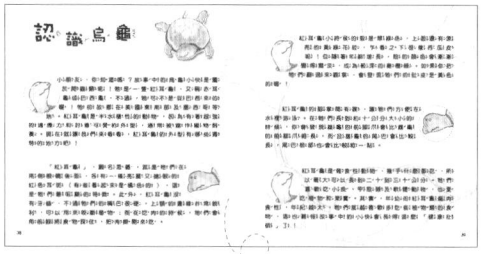

補充與故事有關的小常識，讓讀者更了解故事內容

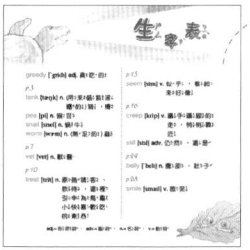

附英文生字表，幫助讀者了解故事內容

小老鼠貝貝歷險記系列

Tabitha and the Elephants

Marc Ponomareff　著／王平，倪靖，郜欣　繪／本局編輯部　譯

精裝／附中英雙語朗讀CD／全套六本

一隻機智勇敢的小老鼠，一隻真誠可愛的象寶寶，
六本為孩子量身打造的雙語繪本，
讓你在一連串驚險刺激的冒險故事中學英文！

① Tabitha Meets An Elephant　貝貝與小潔的相遇
② Tabitha and the Laughing Hyenas　小老鼠貝貝與土狼
③ Tabitha and the Python　小老鼠貝貝與大蟒蛇
④ Tabitha and the Crocodile　小老鼠貝貝與鱷魚
⑤ Tabitha Escapes from the Lions　小老鼠貝貝逃生記
⑥ A Party for Tabitha　小老鼠貝貝的驚喜派對

國家圖書館出版品預行編目資料

Speedy the Greedy Turtle: 貪吃的烏龜小快 / Jill McDougall著;王祖民繪;本局編輯部譯. －－初版一刷. －－臺北市: 三民, 2005
面; 公分. －－(Fun心讀雙語叢書. 小烏龜, 大麻煩系列①)
中英對照
ISBN 957-14-4323-9 (精裝)
1. 英國語言－讀本
523.38 94012414

網路書店位址 http://www.sanmin.com.tw

© Speedy the Greedy Turtle
——貪吃的烏龜小快

著作人 Jill McDougall
繪 者 王祖民
譯 者 本局編輯部
發行人 劉振強
著作財產權人 三民書局股份有限公司
臺北市復興北路386號
發行所 三民書局股份有限公司
地址／臺北市復興北路386號
電話／(02)25006600
郵撥／0009998-5
印刷所 三民書局股份有限公司
門市部 復北店／臺北市復興北路386號
重南店／臺北市重慶南路一段61號
初版一刷 2005年8月
編 號 S 805581
定 價 新臺幣壹佰捌拾元整
行政院新聞局登記證局版臺業字第〇二〇〇號

有著作權・不准侵害

ISBN 957-14-4323-9 (精裝)